The Boxcar Children Mysteries

The Boxcar Children
Surprise Island
The Yellow House Mystery
Mystery Ranch
Mike's Mystery
Blue Bay Mystery
The Woodshed Mystery
The Lighthouse Mystery
The Mountain Top Mystery
Schoolhouse Mystery
Caboose Mystery
Houseboat Mystery
Snowbound Mystery
Tree House Mystery
Bicycle Mystery
Mystery in the Sand
Bus Station Mystery
Benny Uncovers a Mystery
The Haunted Cabin Mystery
The Deserted Library Mystery
The Animal Shelter Mystery
The Old Motel Mystery
The Mystery of the Hidden Painting
The Amusement Park Mystery
The Mystery of the Mixed-Up Zoo
The Camp-Out Mystery
The Mystery Girl
The Mystery Cruise
The Disappearing Friend Mystery
The Mystery of the Singing Ghost
Mystery in the Snow
The Pizza Mystery
The Mystery Horse
The Mystery at the Dog Show
The Castle Mystery
The Mystery of the Lost Village
The Mystery on the Ice
The Mystery of the Purple Pool
The Ghost Ship Mystery
The Mystery in Washington, DC
The Canoe Trip Mystery
The Mystery of the Hidden Beach
The Mystery of the Missing Cat
The Mystery at Snowflake Inn
The Mystery on Stage
The Dinosaur Mystery
The Mystery of the Stolen Music

THE MYSTERY AT THE BALL PARK
THE CHOCOLATE SUNDAE MYSTERY
THE MYSTERY OF THE HOT AIR BALLOON
THE MYSTERY BOOKSTORE
THE PILGRIM VILLAGE MYSTERY
THE MYSTERY OF THE STOLEN BOXCAR
MYSTERY IN THE CAVE
THE MYSTERY ON THE TRAIN
THE MYSTERY AT THE FAIR
THE MYSTERY OF THE LOST MINE
THE GUIDE DOG MYSTERY
THE HURRICANE MYSTERY
THE PET SHOP MYSTERY
THE MYSTERY OF THE SECRET MESSAGE
THE FIREHOUSE MYSTERY
THE MYSTERY IN SAN FRANCISCO
THE NIAGARA FALLS MYSTERY

THE NIAGARA FALLS MYSTERY

created by

GERTRUDE CHANDLER WARNER

Illustrated by Charles Tang

ALBERT WHITMAN & Company
Morton Grove, Illinois

Activities by Nancy E. Krulik
Activity illustrations by Alfred Giuliani

ISBN 0-8075-5603-3

1 3 5 7 9 10 8 6 4 2

Printed in the U.S.A.

Contents

CHAPTER 1

Thundering Waters

"Wake up, everyone. We're getting close!" James Alden said, as he drove along a winding highway. But his four sleepy grandchildren didn't stir.

Mr. Alden lowered the car windows. The fresh air awakened the children one by one. "Can you hear that sound?" he asked.

Six-year-old Benny Alden sat straight up. He never liked to miss a thing. "What is it, Grandfather?"

"That's millions of gallons of water thundering into the Niagara River," Grandfather Alden said. "We're still a few miles away, but you can already hear the falls. All that water is moving toward Niagara Falls, exactly where we're headed."

Benny could see the rushing river from the car window. "It's going so fast."

Jessie Alden, who was twelve, yawned and took a deep gulp of fresh air. "Niagara Falls sounds louder than the ocean."

Fourteen-year-old Henry Alden was awake, too. As he often did on family car trips, Henry was helping his grandfather with directions. "Just think what the falls must sound like up close!"

"We'll have to shout to hear each other," Benny yelled.

Benny's voice woke up his ten-year-old sister, Violet. She leaned toward the open window to enjoy the sunshine. "The river looks like a pretty ribbon cutting through the riverbanks. It reminds me of the stream that was near our old boxcar."

The four Alden children had once lived

alone in a boxcar in the woods. Then their grandfather found them. He took them to live with him in his big house in Greenfield.

Jessie pushed her long brown hair behind her ears. She opened the guidebook on her lap. "It may look like a pretty ribbon, but it's awfully strong. This book says those tall electric towers over there carry electricity from the falls to places all over North America," she said.

"Wow!" Benny said, amazed. "That sounds neat, but most of all, I want to see those boats. You know, the ones that go right near the falls and everybody gets wet? What are they called?"

Violet smiled. "The Maid of the Mist boats, Benny."

Grandfather Alden slowed down to check a sign. "Well, children, it won't be long before you'll actually see those boats. There's the sign for the border between the United States and Canada. In just a few minutes, we'll be in another country."

"Canada, here we come!" Henry said.

Benny could hardly wait. "If we get out of the car, would we be able to put one foot in America and one foot in Canada, Grandfather?"

Mr. Alden chuckled. "Almost. I suppose when we pass through the customs booth, the front of the car will be in Canada, and the back will be in the United States. We could be in two different countries at the same time! Do you know what customs is, Benny?"

"It's where we have to show the people in Canada our birth certificates. What if they don't let us in?" Benny asked. He decided he'd better have something else to show the customs people, just in case.

"Well, let's find out," Grandfather said. He pulled behind a line of cars stopped on a bridge. "This is the Peace Bridge. That customs booth down at the other end of the bridge is on the Canadian side."

The Alden children looked around while they waited for the cars in front of them to pass through the booths.

Violet pointed to a car covered with streamers and trailing noisy soda cans. "I think that couple just got married."

Mr. Alden gave the couple in the car a friendly wave. His grandchildren did the same.

" 'Niagara Falls has been a popular honeymoon spot for over a century,' " Jessie read from her guidebook. " 'Many couples pose for pictures in front of the mists and rainbows that often appear in the falls.' "

Finally, it was the Aldens' turn. A friendly man in a booth looked into the car. "You folks here for business or vacation?"

Mr. Alden showed the man his driver's license and the children's birth certificates. "Business *and* vacation. I'm heading to Ottawa on business. My grandchildren here will be sightseeing and visiting Lasalle's Curiosity Shop. It's owned by an old friend of mine."

"Lasalle's is famous around here," the man said. "They sell all types of souvenirs. You kids will love it! My kids can spend hours in there. Now don't get me going, or we'll back up the cars behind you on the bridge. Okay. Drive through. Welcome to Canada."

Benny couldn't sit still. "I can show you where I live," he said to the customs man. He waved his library card. "In Greenfield."

The customs man smiled. "Well, now that you mention it, young fellow, I'd better check your papers. I need to make sure you're not a spy or anything." He winked at the older children. "Everything seems to be in order," he said. "You are officially in Canada."

Benny waved out the back window. "Good-bye, United States."

"Here's the visitors' center, Grandfather," Henry announced a few minutes later. "We could use some local maps."

Mr. Alden drove slowly through the crowded parking lot. The children took turns reading the names of states from license plates.

"Montana," Henry said.

"That's the third Montana plate we've

seen," Violet reminded Henry. "But look. There's a car from Alaska — the first one we've seen. And it's a honeymoon car, too, with streamers and all."

Finally the children got out of the car and stretched their legs. It had been a long trip from their house in Greenfield all the way to Canada.

Benny skipped ahead into the visitors' center. Right away he saw what he was looking for — dozens of brochures for the travel scrapbook he and Violet kept. "Too bad we can't stay a long, long time." He scooped up ads for hotels, restaurants, horse-and-buggy rides and, of course, the famous Maid of the Mist boats.

Jessie showed Benny a brochure of a tower with a restaurant on top. "Here's a restaurant that spins around. You can look at the falls while you eat."

Henry patted his stomach. "I'm not sure I want to spin while I eat. I wonder if there's a brochure for Lasalle's Curiosity Shop. Hey, there's a bunch," he said when he spotted some ads on display shelves in the lobby. "I'll pick one up so we can find out exactly where the shop is."

Just as Henry reached for one of the brochures, someone snatched all of them away.

"Hey," Henry said to the tall blond young man hurrying away. "Why don't you leave some for other people?"

The man rushed off without turning around.

"Let's follow him," Jessie said to Henry when she saw what had happened. "I'm sure he didn't mean to take all of them."

Jessie ran after the man, but he had disappeared into the crowd.

Henry scratched his head. "Why would anyone need a stack of ads from Lasalle's? Those are the only ones he took."

Jessie came back. "It *is* odd. Maybe he works for a hotel or a tour bus company and picked them up for the customers."

The children walked on. They stopped at the water fountain to refill their water bottles. Jessie noticed something in the trash basket nearby.

"Hey, look! That man didn't take the brochures for customers. He dumped them all in this trash basket."

Henry and Jessie scooped up the brochures. Jessie marched over to the display case. She restacked the brochures under *L* for *Lasalle's.* "I wonder why that man threw them out. Well, anyway, now they're back where visitors will see them."

When the children returned to the car, they told their grandfather about the tall man and the missing brochures.

"That is quite curious," Grandfather told the children after he started the car. "Come to think of it, a tall young fellow left the parking lot in a hurry about ten minutes ago. He drove a brown car, I believe. He was in such a hurry that he almost brushed against a parked car. We should mention the missing fliers to Will Lasalle. He's minding the shop while his grandfather is away in Toronto."

"Anyway, we did get a brochure, after all, and this free map, too, Grandfather," Henry

said. "Now we've got exact directions to the shop from here."

Mr. Alden kept his eye on the traffic. "It's on Waterfall Street, not far from the Maid of the Mist docks."

Henry looked at the map, then up ahead. "Take a right turn here, Grandfather, onto the Niagara River Parkway for a couple miles. We'll be able to see the Canadian Falls."

"We're almost there!" Benny shouted, his eyes glued to the river running next to the highway. "The river is moving even faster now."

Grandfather Alden watched the road while Henry checked the map. "Look, there's Goat Island. It separates the American Falls from Horseshoe Falls on the Canadian side," Henry told everyone.

The traffic slowed as the Aldens got closer to Horseshoe Falls. Mr. Alden signaled right. "There's a lookout here. You children are about to get your first view of the falls."

Everyone scrambled out of the car as

soon as Mr. Alden pulled into the lookout and turned off the engine. The children couldn't wait to see what was making the huge roar.

The four children gasped when they stepped onto the lookout deck. Horseshoe Falls lay directly ahead, crashing down to the rocks and river below.

"The Canadian Falls really are curved like a horseshoe," Jessie shouted above the roar.

Violet tapped her brothers and sister when she noticed something special. She pointed to a perfect rainbow that appeared in the clouds of mist blowing off the falls.

"Amazing," Henry said when everyone got back in the car.

"We were so lucky to see a rainbow on our first day in Niagara Falls," Violet said. "You can only see a rainbow in the mist if it's sunny like today. Thank you for stopping, Grandfather."

"I knew you children would love it here," Grandfather Alden said.

CHAPTER 2

A Mysterious Message

As the Aldens rode through the town of Niagara Falls, they saw colorful signs outside motels, hotels, and inns inviting honeymooners, families, and everyone else to come and stay awhile.

"There's Waterfall Street," Henry announced shortly after the Aldens passed the Maid of the Mist docks.

Grandfather searched for a parking place. "That's odd. Lasalle's should be right on this block. Do you see a sign for it, Henry?"

There were many shops on Waterfall Street, but Lasalle's Curiosity Shop was nowhere to be seen.

"Let's pull into this parking space," Grandfather said. "I know the shop is here somewhere."

Benny got out of the car and ran ahead. He finally stopped in front of a shop. The first person he saw was an older man with a long white beard sitting on a bench. On the sidewalk was a banged-up suitcase displaying small pieces of wood inside.

"What are those?" Benny asked the man.

The man didn't answer. Instead he handed Benny a piece of paper.

Benny showed Jessie the paper. "What does this say? The words are too long for me to read."

Jessie looked at the flier. On it was an old-fashioned photo of a woman standing next to a large wooden barrel. Jessie read the information to Benny.

"Hettie Drummond stands next to the barrel in which she went over the falls in 1905. These

pieces of wood are part of the barrel that survived the falls along with Mrs. Drummond. The pieces can be purchased for a dollar apiece."

Benny, who loved collecting souvenirs, dug into his pocket for his cowboy wallet. "I have a dollar from our paper route. I'd like to buy one, Grandfather."

"Go right ahead, Benny," Mr. Alden said. "This will be a nice addition to your souvenir collection."

Benny handed the bearded man a dollar. "May I pick any piece?"

The man nodded but didn't speak.

Benny studied the small wooden souvenirs. Finally he found a curved piece that was a little bit worn down. "This piece sure looks like it went down Niagara Falls," he said. "I'll take it."

Benny handed the man his dollar, then tucked the souvenir into the pocket of his jeans.

"Sir, I wonder if you could point us to Lasalle's Curiosity Shop," Mr. Alden said to the bearded man.

The bearded man still didn't speak. Finally he turned around. He pointed to the store right behind him.

Grandfather Alden tapped his forehead. "It was right in front of us the whole time! I wonder why there's no sign."

Before entering the shop, Benny turned around to speak to the bearded man. "Thanks for the souvenir."

The bearded man smiled. "You're welcome, sonny. This is the first one I've sold in quite a while."

Lasalle's Curiosity Shop was even better than Mr. Alden had told his grandchildren. It was crowded with souvenirs and goodies. Banners, posters, postcards, T-shirts, Maid of the Mist model boats, Native American crafts, and guidebooks filled the store. And the treats! Benny could hardly take his eyes off the fudge, taffy, and peppermint sticks that filled the old-fashioned jars.

But despite all the wonderful things in the shop, there wasn't a customer in sight.

"Hello, hello," Mr. Alden called out when

he didn't see anyone minding the store.

Finally someone appeared from the back of the shop.

"Hello, there," a friendly dark-haired young man said when he saw the Aldens. "May I help you with something?"

Mr. Alden put out his hand. "I bet you don't recognize me, do you, Will?"

At first the young man looked puzzled. Then he broke into a grin. "Are you James Alden? Granddad told me you and your grandchildren would be arriving today. Now I recognize you from some family photos taken when my cousin Michel and I were six years old."

Mr. Alden smiled at the young man. "Exactly right! Why, when I was here fifteen years ago you were the same age as my grandson Benny is now. You're the image of your father and grandfather."

The young man grinned again. "That's what everyone says. Michel takes after my grandmother's side. Do you remember him?"

Mr. Alden nodded. "I certainly do. You

boys were more like brothers than cousins. Is Michel helping you out with the shop while your grandfather is away?"

Will Lasalle's smile faded. "No . . . not anymore."

Mr. Alden could see the young man was upset about his cousin. He changed the subject. "Let me introduce you to my grandchildren. Meet Benny, Violet, Jessie, and Henry. Children, meet Will Lasalle. He was the same size as you, Benny, the last time I visited Niagara Falls."

"I'm a little taller now," Will joked when the children held out their hands for handshakes. "I haven't had this many customers for a few days. Our sign blew off a couple of nights ago and got damaged. That has slowed down business quite a bit. Did you have trouble finding the shop?"

"A little, since we didn't see a sign," Henry began. "And the other thing. Somebody took all the Lasalle's brochures from the visitors' center, then threw them out. But Jessie put them back."

Will Lasalle looked troubled. "I just

dropped off piles of brochures all around Niagara Falls yesterday. Ever since my grandfather left, the brochures keep disappearing. We depend on those ads to get new customers in here."

Jessie had one of her good ideas. "We'll be sightseeing all over Niagara Falls. If you give us some brochures, we'll be sure to leave plenty of them wherever we go."

"I'll take you up on that," Will said. "I've been pretty busy with the shop. I also work part-time on the Maid of the Mist boats."

Benny was thrilled by this piece of news. "You work on those boats? Is it scary?" he asked.

Will Lasalle chuckled. "It's an exciting ride, Benny, but not too scary. The Maid of the Mist boats have been carrying tourists safely for a long time. We even give passengers rain slickers. The passengers get so close to the falls, they often get wet."

"I know," Benny said, barely containing his enthusiasm. "We heard lots of stories about people going over the falls other ways. And know what?"

"What?" Will Lasalle had no idea what would pop out of Benny's mouth next.

Benny reached into his pocket. He pulled out the scrap of wood he'd bought from the bearded man. "Guess what this is."

Will scratched his head. "I have to confess. It just looks like an old piece of wood."

Benny shook his head. "Not any old piece of wood. It's part of a barrel that a lady rode inside of when she went over the falls a long, long time ago. I bought it from a man with a white beard."

Will walked over to the store window. He knocked on the glass. The Aldens saw the bearded man outside, but he didn't turn around.

"That's Angus Drummond," Will explained. "He sets up outside the different shops and tries to sell people bits and pieces of the old barrel one of his ancestors went down the falls in. He's full of stories."

"He didn't say much to us at all," Jessie said.

"Angus can sometimes be shy around strangers," Will told the Aldens. "But he knows everything there is to know about Niagara Falls. My grandfather often invites Angus in for advice about his collection of antique souvenirs. We keep them in the display room that connects to the shop. It's closed now. I haven't had enough help to fix it up and keep it open to visitors."

Will Lasalle stopped talking to answer the phone. "Yes, they just got here, Granddad," the Aldens overheard him say. "And I finally hired some people to cover for me when I'm working on the Maid of the Mist. A young couple passing through Niagara Falls on their honeymoon needed some money to continue their wedding trip. They're going to help out for the next few weeks. Don't worry about a thing."

Will listened to his grandfather at the other end before handing the phone to Mr. Alden.

Will turned to the children. "My grandfather is in Toronto for a couple of weeks. I don't know what you think of this, but Granddad wants me to ask you if you'd like to do a few chores around the shop — just part-time. You'd still have plenty of time for sightseeing."

Will could see by their eager faces that the Aldens were excited already. "The display room next to the shop needs a good cleanup. There are quite a few boxes full of things that need to be unpacked and put on display. I could sure use four more pairs of hands around here. Any chance you'd be interested?"

The children looked at each other. Who wouldn't be interested in working in Niagara Falls?

"Can we work in the shop, Grandfather?" Benny asked when Mr. Alden got off the phone. "Will just asked us to."

"Wouldn't you like to just take a plain old vacation for a change?" Mr. Alden asked, even though he knew what the answer would be.

"Working in this neat shop would be

better than any plain old vacation," Henry said.

Will Lasalle looked at Mr. Alden. "They'll still have plenty of time for sightseeing. As I told my grandfather, I just hired a couple to work in the souvenir shop for the next few weeks. Granddad said your grandchildren could help out with our display room. And one other thing. The couple I hired will be staying in the apartment above the shop. If you'd like, the children can stay in the bungalow behind the shop. The couple can keep an eye on them when I'm not here." Will noticed how puzzled Benny was. "The bungalow's a small cottage my granddad built."

"Then that settles it," Mr. Alden said. "Working seems to be my grandchildren's idea of a vacation."

"When do we start?" Henry and Jessie asked at the same time.

"How about tomorrow morning after breakfast?" Will suggested. "I'll have the bungalow ready. You can work in the morning, then go sightseeing in the afternoon."

Mr. Alden headed for the door. "I'd better get these children some dinner and a good night's sleep if they're going to be working. We're staying at the Rainbow Inn tonight."

"I'll meet you here at eight tomorrow morning," Will said. "Now it's time to close up. I've got to head over to the Maid of the Mist. I'll follow you out."

Everyone looked for Angus Drummond outside, but there was no sign of him anywhere.

"Do you think we'll see Mr. Drummond again?" Violet asked. "I'd like to hear some of the old stories he tells about Niagara Falls. Maybe he knows the Maid of the Mist tale."

"He knows every story ever told about Niagara Falls," Will said as he unlocked his car door. "Angus'll be around, all right. He likes to drop in the shop just to look around. I guess I'll see you folks tomorrow morning. If I'm going to make the last ride of the day I have to get going," he said before he drove off.

After Will left, Grandfather unlocked his car. Then he noticed a piece of paper under the windshield. "Goodness. I got a parking ticket. I completely forgot to put money in the parking meter."

Henry lifted the wiper blade and picked up the piece of paper. "Well, Grandfather, it looks as if we have another Canadian souvenir. Hey, wait! It's not a parking ticket at all. It's some kind of flier. Look, most of the other cars have these fliers on them, too."

"What does it say?"

Henry held the paper under the street lamp. "It says: 'Going Out of Business. Lasalle's Curiosity Shop. Closing for good April twenty-ninth.' "

"Impossible," Mr. Alden said. "That's tomorrow. Let's follow Will and show him this."

Everyone hurried into the car. Mr. Alden drove straight to the Maid of the Mist docks. The Aldens searched all over for

Will Lasalle, but they were too late. The last boat had already gone out, and Will Lasalle was on it.

"We missed him," Jessie said. "Let's take the fliers off all the cars ourselves. It can't be true that the shop is closing tomorrow. Will just hired us and that couple to work there. It's not possible."

Grandfather Alden drove back to Waterfall Street. Now that it was getting dark, the street was quiet. One by one, the Aldens removed the fliers from the cars. Whoever played this practical joke wasn't going to get away with it — not if the Aldens could help it.

"Who would do such a mean thing?" Violet asked.

"Whoever did this doesn't seem to be around," Henry said after they removed the last flier.

But Henry was wrong. The person who had placed the fliers on the cars was watching the Aldens from the shadows.

CHAPTER 3

Someone Plays a Trick

Except for the Aldens, all the tables in the breakfast room of the Rainbow Inn were filled with happy couples.

"This is such a romantic place," Jessie said. "I saw a couple holding hands by the fireplace last night."

"We're the only big family," Benny announced after he finished his orange juice. "I like the Rainbow Inn, but I'm glad we're going to a real house today — where we won't have to watch that romance stuff. Yuck!"

Mr. Alden put down his coffee cup. "Are you sure that's what you children want to do? Mr. Lumberton, the innkeeper invited you to stay at the Rainbow Inn for as long as you'd like. You can have their famous peach pie every day."

For a second, Benny almost changed his mind. "Every day?"

Henry put an end to that. "We can buy pies at the bakery on Waterfall Street, Benny. Don't you want to work at Lasalle's Curiosity Shop?"

Benny took another sip of juice before answering. "As long as I get more pie."

"We'll make sure of that, Benny," Jessie said. "Let's finish up these pancakes. This maple syrup tastes as if it just came from the trees."

The Aldens had just finished breakfast when they heard loud voices outside the dining room.

"But couldn't we stay the rest of the week?" a teary-eyed young woman with long dark hair asked Mr. Lumberton. "We have jobs now. We could pay you on Friday. We're on our honeymoon."

Mr. Lumberton shook his head, sad to turn down the young woman. "I'm sorry, but that's our policy. As it is, you still owe us for two nights."

The tall blond young man standing next to the woman looked upset. "We left our name and where we'll be. We'll have all the money by next week. We expected a check at our wedding, but it didn't arrive. Now that we have jobs, we can pay for the last two nights and the rest of this week as soon as we get paid."

Mr. Lumberton's mind was made up. "I'm sorry, Mr. and Mrs. McKenzie, but you'll have to leave. You're welcome back once you pay for the two nights and give us a deposit for a longer stay." Mr. Lumberton rang the desk bell. "Please bring Mr. and Mrs. McKenzie's luggage out to their car," Mr. Lumberton said to a clerk.

"Too bad they have to leave," Violet whispered. "They looked so happy at dinner last night. I saw them holding hands at the table by the fireplace."

The Aldens finished breakfast. Then they checked out of the Rainbow Inn, too.

"Look, they're taking down the JUST MARRIED sign from the back of their car," Jessie said when she saw the couple outside. "How sad."

The Aldens got in their car and followed the couple's old brown car from the parking lot of the inn. Only one banged-up can trailing from the couple's car bumper gave any sign that the young man and woman were on their honeymoon. The brown car took a turn toward the falls. The Aldens went up Waterfall Street.

"Look! Those fliers are on all the cars again!" Violet said. "Somebody must have come back after we left."

Sure enough, nearly every car parked on Waterfall Street had a "Going-Out-of-Business" flier under its windshield again. The children wasted no time removing the fliers.

When the children returned, Grandfather Alden knocked on the shop door. There was no answer. "It's quarter to eight. We're early. I'll wait until Will gets here to get to the bottom of this."

The children wouldn't hear of it.

"You don't have to stay, Grandfather," Jessie said. "We'll figure out how these fliers got on the cars."

Mr. Alden checked his watch. "Then I will get going. It's a long way to Ottawa. Let's unload your suitcases and the cooler."

"Okay, I'll help you," Henry said, grabbing two pieces of luggage.

"Good-bye, Grandfather," the children called out when Mr. Alden's car pulled away.

The parking spot wasn't empty for long, though. Will Lasalle pulled into it almost as soon as Grandfather left. "Hey, what's the matter?" he asked when he noticed the children looked upset about something.

Jessie handed Will one of the fliers. "These 'Going-Out-of Business' notices were on the cars this morning again."

"What do you mean, 'again'?" Will asked.

"Last night there was one on our windshield and on most of the other cars on the street," Henry explained. "So we took them off. We tried to find you, but you were already on the boat. Somebody put more fliers on these cars after we left."

Will's brown eyes filled with worry. "Who can be doing this? First I lost my store sign. Next I found out that somebody's throwing away all our ads. Now these fliers. What's going on?"

"Maybe we can find out," Benny said.

For the first time that morning, Will Lasalle smiled a little. "If anyone can figure this out, I know it's you Aldens. Let me get you settled in the bungalow. Then I'll come back and show you around our display room," Will said, leading the children down a short passageway on the side of the shop. "I'll be back in a while."

"It's like a miniature cabin," Violet said when Will let everyone into a snug cottage in back of the shop.

"Granddad built this bungalow by hand," Will explained. "The walls are made of Canadian logs. The stones for the fireplace came from the farm where he grew up. And those snowshoes on the wall belonged to my great uncle."

"It's cozy — just what we like," Jessie said as she carried the cooler into the kitchen. "This is just as nice as the Rainbow Inn."

"Except for the peach pie," Benny reminded his sister.

Will went to the door. "Why don't you unpack while I open up the shop. Then I'll show you around. I'll leave the back door to the display room unlocked. See you in a while."

After Will left, the Aldens opened the windows to let in some fresh air. Henry and Benny put away the food from their cooler. Mrs. McGregor, Mr. Aldens' housekeeper, knew how hungry four children could get. She always packed a cooler with some of her delicious home-cooked food for their car trips.

"Listen," Henry said when he heard voices out back. "I think our neighbors are here."

The children overheard Will talking to some people as they climbed the stairs behind the shop.

"That must be the couple he hired," Jessie said. "I hope they're nice. I don't know about the rest of you, but I'm ready to start work."

"Me, too," Violet said.

"Me, three," Benny said, laughing.

The children walked outside, and Henry locked the door to the bungalow. Will had left the back door to the display room open. The second the children got inside, they heard something.

"Somebody's in here!" Henry whispered. "I thought Will was upstairs showing the couple the apartment."

Jessie followed the sound of footsteps into the shop area that connected to the display room. "Who's there?" she called.

The only answer was the shop door slamming. The children caught a glimpse of someone on the sidewalk.

"Let's follow whoever it is," Henry suggested.

By the time the children got outside, all they saw was a dark brown car driving down the street. Across the way, Angus Drummond sat quietly with his suitcase in front of him.

Violet waved, but Angus didn't look up.

"Do you think Angus was in here?" Jessie asked Henry when everyone returned to the shop.

Henry shook his head. "I'm not sure. He looks like he's been sitting there for a while. Maybe it was a delivery person."

While the Aldens were still discussing the intruder, Will walked in.

"Guess what?" Benny asked, bursting with news. "We just chased somebody out of the display room."

Will looked puzzled. "Somebody was in there? You don't mean the couple I hired, do you? I brought them upstairs so they could settle in before they start work later today. The husband just left to pick up my new store sign. Maybe he took a shortcut through the shop."

"I think you were all still upstairs," Henry

explained. "The person who was in the display room went through the shop and out the front door. Were you expecting a delivery?"

Will shook his head. "Not this early. Hmmm. It's possible one of my suppliers came by and dropped something off. But I don't see any packages."

"Whoever it was got out of here fast," Jessie said. "Anyway, we're in a hurry, too — to get to work."

Will looked around. "Well, everything seems to be in place, so I'm not going to worry. I'm just glad you're all here to give me a hand. Follow me."

Will led the Aldens into the display room. He turned on the light. "This room is Granddad's pride and joy," Will explained. "He's been collecting antiques and oddities from around Niagara Falls his whole life. We usually get a lot of tourists in here — people who want to know about the history of Niagara Falls. Most of the things in this room are one of a kind."

The room was a jumble of dusty treasures. Old photographs hung on the walls. Postcard albums lay open on the counters. A tag on a section of metal cable explained that it was part of the first cable bridge built across the Niagara River. Two barrels stood in the corner with signs describing the people who had gone over the falls in them.

Benny pointed up to the ceiling where a long curved wooden pole hung from corner to corner. "What's that?"

"That's a balancing pole a famous tightrope walker used in 1859 to cross over the river down by Whirlpool Rapids. The rapids are pretty dangerous. This pole is the most famous item in my grandfather's collection, except for one."

Will walked over to a glass display case in the center of the room. He turned on the overhead light. "Hey! Why is this case unlocked?" he asked. "Maybe Granddad was in a rush and forgot to close it. I wouldn't want anybody to get his hands on this guest book. It's pretty valuable."

The children came over to see what Will was talking about.

"It's just a plain old book," Benny said, a little disappointed. The balancing pole on the ceiling was a lot more exciting.

"It's not just a plain old book, Benny," Will began. "It's a priceless guest book from a hotel my great-great-grandparents owned. When the Prince of Wales visited Niagara Falls in 1860, he stayed at their hotel and signed this book. It's been in our family for over a hundred and thirty years."

"Is it usually locked up?" Jessie asked.

"Always," Will answered. "In fact, the insurance company keeps telling Granddad he should keep it in a safe or at a bank. But he won't hear of it. He wants to share these treasures with visitors who come to the shop. Granddad must have left the case unlocked by mistake. Good thing I noticed. I'll lock it up now."

Will was walking toward a cabinet in the corner of the room when he accidentally kicked something. "Gosh! Granddad really must have been rushed. He dropped these keys. I'd better lock up the guest book case right now." He turned the key in the lock and rechecked it twice before putting the keys into his pocket.

For the next half hour, Will showed the Aldens where things were and what to do. Everything needed a good vacuuming. Boxes needed to be unpacked. A list needed to be written to keep track of everything.

"Is that too much work?" he asked the children a while later.

"For us?" Benny asked. "Nothing's too much work!"

"Let's get going," Jessie said.

CHAPTER 4

A Wallet Disappears

"*Achoo!*" Violet sneezed for the third time in a row while she was vacuuming. "There's an awful lot of dust in here."

By late morning there was less dust but still quite a few boxes stacked up in the display room.

"Tomorrow we can start unpacking," Jessie said. "When we're done, this room will be like a little museum."

As the children worked, a few customers peeked into the display room.

"Too bad this room is closed," one man

from a tour bus said when he and his wife stepped into the display room by mistake. "We honeymooned in Niagara Falls fifty years ago. We just love looking back on how it was in the old days."

Henry smiled at the couple. "If you come back in a couple of days, this room will be open again."

After the couple left, the children continued with their work. Henry had just piled some empty boxes near the connecting doorway to the shop when he noticed something. "That man dropped his wallet!" Henry ran through the shop after the couple. He was too late. Their tour bus had just pulled away.

Henry stood on the sidewalk and checked inside the wallet. "Wow! There's over three hundred dollars in here. And some identification cards, too."

Back inside, Will Lasalle was showing a young couple how to use the cash register. Before Henry had a chance to tell about the lost wallet, Will waved Henry over.

"Henry, bring Benny and your sisters out

here," Will said. "I want everyone to meet my new assistant managers."

When the Aldens came into the shop area, Will introducd everyone. "These are the Aldens: Benny, Violet, Jessie, and Henry. Kids, I'd like you to meet Robert and Sally McKenzie."

The children smiled at the McKenzies before glancing at each other.

"You children look as if you have a little secret," Will said with a smile. "Come on. Let us in on it."

Benny couldn't hold it in. "We saw you on your honeymoon at the Rainbow Inn. Only we weren't on a honeymoon — just a regular trip."

Will chuckled. He didn't notice that the McKenzies weren't smiling at all.

Jessie poked Benny gently with her elbow. "Sorry. We weren't snooping on you at the Rainbow Inn. It's just that we were the only family there that *wasn't* on a honeymoon."

Robert McKenzie still looked upset, but Sally McKenzie seemed to relax a bit. "It's okay. I bet it feels strange to be around so many couples when you're with your whole family."

"Well, this family is helping me organize the display room next door. We plan to reopen it soon," Will explained. "It's gotten pretty dusty and disorganized. I asked the Aldens to straighten things out for us. It'll be shipshape when my grandfather returns."

Robert McKenzie didn't seem too happy to hear this. "No need for these kids to give up their vacation. Sally and I can fix up the display room in our spare time. I thought that's why you hired us — so we could take care of everything while you're working on the Maid of the Mist."

"Oh, I'll need you in the shop and running errands for me," Will said. "Picking up my store sign this morning was a big help already. There's more than enough work for everyone."

Mr. McKenzie seemed about to say something until his wife gave him a funny look.

The Aldens walked back to the display room when Henry remembered something.

"Oh! I almost forgot why I came out here in the first place. A couple from the tour bus dropped this wallet when they were talking to us. What should I do with it?"

Will took the wallet and put it into a drawer. "Granddad keeps lost items locked in this drawer near the cash register for a day or so in case the owner comes back. If no one does, then we take the item to the Lost and Found Department at the police station. Most times, folks figure out where they lost it and come right back."

Henry was relieved. "I hope this couple comes back. There's a few hundred dollars in there and the man's identification cards." He turned to the McKenzies. "Let us know if you need any help."

Mrs. McKenzie was about to say something when her husband spoke up first. "No, we can handle everything out here, no question about that."

Will said good-bye to the McKenzies and the Aldens. "You've got the keys to the cash register and the lost and found drawer. Lasalle's Curiosity Shop is in good hands.

Now I'd better get down to the Maid of the Mist docks. The next boat departs in a half hour. So long."

" 'Bye," the Aldens said before they went back to work.

Minutes later, Robert McKenzie appeared in the doorway. "We have to shut this door between the store and this room. It's hard to hear ourselves think with all the noise."

Jessie blinked nervously. "Oh! Sorry. We didn't know we were so noisy. Talking makes the work go faster. We'll be quieter."

Without another word, Mr. McKenzie slammed the door anyway.

"Gee," Violet said, biting her lip. "For someone who just got married, he seems very cross. I guess he's upset about leaving the Rainbow Inn. Maybe he knows we overheard them talking about their money problems."

Jessie sighed. "That's probably true, Violet. We'll just have to be as nice as we can. I don't want the McKenzies to feel unhappy around us. Still, I wish we could keep the door open. We'd get to know each other better if we worked side by side."

Henry got curious about a long skinny box he found. He lifted the lid. Inside were several odd-looking wooden canes. "Hmm, I have no idea why these are in here. There aren't any tags or notes explaining what they are."

Jessie came over and twirled one of the canes. "I wonder how these connect to Niagara Falls. Maybe they're part of some costumes from an old musical or something."

"What nonsense," a gruff voice said from the corner of the room.

Startled, the Aldens turned in the direction of the voice.

"Everybody around here knows those canes weren't used onstage," the gruff voice said.

"Mr. Drummond!" Jessie cried. "We didn't see you. How did you get in here?"

Angus Drummond stepped from a dark corner into the middle of the room. "Same way I always get in here. Right through the back door. I've been here the whole time you were yammering out in the shop. Now hand me that cane, young lady. I'll show you what a real Niagara Falls souvenir is."

Angus Drummond wasn't too friendly-looking. His clothes were a bit worn. His white beard hadn't been trimmed in quite a while. But now that the Aldens knew who belonged to the gruff voice, they weren't afraid of him.

Angus took the cane from Jessie and held it up. "Now, this is a fine-looking Navy Island cane. Probably fifty years old if it's a day. Even older, I reckon. And do you know where this cane was made?"

Before the Aldens could answer, Angus's voice boomed out: "Niagara Falls, that's where! These canes are made from trees on Navy Island, smack in the middle of the Niagara River. There was a time when nearly every tourist walked around with one of these."

"Were these canes carved by hand?" Violet asked. "They look very well made."

Angus's voice boomed again. "Of course they were made by hand, young lady. There

was a workshop on the river where woodcarvers turned these canes out by the thousands. No more, though. All folks want now are a lot of T-shirts and caps and other ugly nonsense."

"We'll put the canes in a special place," Jessie told Angus. "I'll make a sign explaining what they are. Maybe you can come back tomorrow and tell me what the sign should say."

Angus ran his hand over the wooden cane. "It should just say: NAVY ISLAND CANES. HANDMADE IN NIAGARA FALLS. And make sure you keep 'em in a case. They're worth some money. Not as much as the Prince of Wales guest book, of course. Nothing in this shop is worth as much as that. All the same, those Navy Island canes are valuable."

Violet smiled at Angus Drummond. "Don't worry. We'll put them where everyone can see them."

Jessie laid the canes back in the box. "I hope you can return tomorrow morning. We want to set things up like a museum.

Will you be around, Mr. Drummond?"

Angus nodded. "The name's Angus. That's what folks around here call me. And I'm always around."

"Will told us that," Benny piped up. "And he said you have lots of stories."

Angus nearly smiled. "I've known Willy Lasalle since he was born. Fancy that young fella thinking he can work the Maid of the Mist and run this shop at the same time. He's still wet behind the ears."

"I'm going to be wet behind the ears, too," Benny announced. "We're going on the Maid of the Mist boat. Everything gets wet, even your ears."

This time, Angus Drummond really did smile. "Well, you won't get too wet. They give folks plastic raincoats nowadays, not like in the old days when folks didn't mind getting wet. No, not like the old days."

"I like my piece of barrel from the olden days," Benny said. He pulled his wood piece from his pocket. "See, I still have it."

Angus nodded. "You have a real piece of history there, young fella. My Aunt Tilda went over Horseshoe Falls in 1905 in that barrel — not a scratch on her, either. I asked Will's grandfather to put the barrel on display, but he said he had two already. So I decided to give folks a real souvenir, not these things that fall apart the minute you get home."

Benny held his barrel piece tight in his hands. "Thank you for selling it to me," he said.

Angus smiled directly at Benny. "Thank you for buying it. Not too many folks can appreciate a souvenir like this, young fella. Someday, that will be worth a lot of money."

With that, Angus turned and walked out the back door of the display room — the same way he had come in.

CHAPTER 5

A Face in the Tunnels

Good as his word, Angus Drummond appeared at the back door the next morning. Side by side with Angus, the Aldens unpacked boxes and listened to his stories.

After they'd been working together for a while, Jessie had an idea. "Would you like to come with us to Journey Behind the Falls, Angus? There are tunnels and caves right behind the falls. People stand and watch the falls crash in front of them. Can you come?" she asked.

"No, no," Angus answered. "Many a time I visited those tunnels in the old days before they were all fixed up. In my day, the tunnels were open to the air and water. And if you didn't watch where you were going, you could wind up in the river for good."

"I'm glad it's safer now," Jessie said. "I'm sorry you can't come with us. I guess we'll lock up."

Angus wasn't quite ready to leave, after all. "If you don't mind, I'd like to take another look at some of these things. They've been packed up so long. I'll go out through the store when I'm done."

Jessie gestured for Henry to come into the store with her. "Do you think it's okay if he stays, Henry?" she asked him.

"I think so. He seems nice enough," Henry replied.

Jessie went back into the display room and checked that the back door and all the displays were locked up. "Good-bye. I hope you'll come back tomorrow, Angus."

The children left through the store, leaving the connecting door open. Angus was too busy looking through a box of old photos to answer Jessie or to say good-bye.

The Aldens took a bus from the shop to Table Rock Plaza, where the tunnels were. Joining a long line of people, they bought tickets to Journey Behind the Falls. They joined another line to get the raincoats and boots everyone needed to enter the tunnels.

While waiting, Henry noticed a nearby table filled with fliers. "I brought along some extra brochures from Lasalle's Curiosity Shop," he told the other children. "I'll put some on that table while we wait."

Henry came back empty-handed. "There wasn't a single brochure for the shop. I left all the ones I brought. Either people are picking up an awful lot of brochures or somebody is taking way more than his share. Will told me he left a stack of brochures here just a couple days ago, but they were all gone."

The line of tourists moved slowly. Finally the Aldens got their raincoats and boots. They could hardly wait to get soaked!

"Maybe we can ask someone to take our

pictures in these funny outfits." Jessie reached into her backpack for her instant camera.

She turned to a couple standing behind the children. "Would you like us to take your picture, then you take ours?" Jessie paused when she realized who the couple was. "Aren't you the people who were in Lasalle's Curiosity Shop yesterday? My family works there."

"Yes, we're Mr. and Mrs. Lundy. We met you yesterday," the woman answered. "In fact, we went to the shop about a half hour ago before our tour bus brought us here. We didn't see you children, though, just a young couple. I'm afraid they weren't too helpful about finding the wallet we probably lost in the shop."

"I found your wallet after you left," Henry told the Lundys.

"You know about our wallet?" Mr. Lundy asked. "We did go back for it, but the people who work there said they turned it in to the police."

"Did the police have it?" Henry asked.

"That's just it," Mr. Lundy answered. "The police went through their lost and found box. My wallet wasn't there. Nobody remembered anyone bringing in a wallet. So we took a taxi back to the shop. Then a strange thing happened. As soon as we got out of our taxi, somebody put the CLOSED sign on the door. We've given up on finding it."

Jessie felt sorry for the couple. "Why don't you come back with us after this tour. We might be able to help you. It's probably just a mix-up."

Mrs. Lundy shook her head. "We can't. Right after this tour, our group leaves for Montreal. If we're not on the bus, they'll leave without us. We won't be returning to Niagara Falls."

"There, there, Alice," the man said to his wife. "It's only some money and a few identification cards. They can be replaced."

"I know," the woman said. "It's spoiled our second honeymoon a bit, that's all."

Henry had a good idea. "Why don't you

write down the phone numbers of the places you're staying on the rest of your tour. If we find your wallet, we'll call you and send it to you."

The couple felt better when they heard this. They smiled at the Aldens.

"Stay just like that," Jessie said, "and I'll take your picture." She pressed the camera button. A few minutes later, the instant picture of the smiling couple was ready.

"Your turn," Mr. Lundy said when the Aldens posed for their picture. "Say cheese."

While everyone was waiting for the instant picture to be ready, Mr. Lundy gave Henry a list of the places they'd be staying.

"Thanks," Henry said. "I know we'll find your wallet. Now we'd better all hurry. The line is moving to the elevator that goes down to the tunnels."

Jessie quickly packed up her camera and the photograph. With the others, she boarded the elevator and listened to the guide explain a few rules to follow in the tunnels. Everyone would have a few minutes to look at the falls before moving along so other groups could see them, too.

"Enjoy yourselves. Remember, stay with your group," the guide said before the elevator doors opened.

A few minutes later the Aldens couldn't hear a word. Directly in front of them was a roaring wall of water. The children could hardly believe that they were practically *in* the falls!

Soon it was time to move along. The children followed the guide when he waved everyone back to the elevator. The doors were about to close when the guide stopped. "Sir! Sir!" he called out to someone who had slipped away from the group. "You can't go back that way. Please get on the elevator."

It was no use. The guide's voice was lost in the roar of the nearby falls. Whoever the guide was talking to had joined the next group of tourists already in the tunnels.

After the doors closed, the guide said to

the crowd, "Anyone here missing someone? If so, just wait by the elevator when we get back up, so your companion can find you."

No one on the elevator spoke up.

Jessie tapped Henry on the shoulder. "Did you see who it was?" she asked her brother.

Henry turned around. "It's odd. I had the strangest feeling it was that man we saw at the visitors' center the day we arrived in Canada. But there were so many people in front of me, I couldn't tell. Anyway, whoever it was, he's with the other group down in the tunnel."

When the elevator doors opened, everyone stepped out. The Aldens turned around.

"No one seems to be waiting for the missing person," Henry said. "I guess the man came here by himself. I wish we could wait, but I told Will we'd be back soon. We'd better get going."

Benny wriggled out of his raincoat and boots. "Can Violet and I pick up some brochures for my scrapbook?" he asked Jessie.

"Sure, go ahead," Jessie said. "We'll catch up."

When Violet and Benny checked the table with the free brochures, they looked for new ones they didn't have yet.

"Wait a minute," Violet said. "Where are the brochures Henry just put here? Henry! Henry!" she called out to her brother.

When Henry came over, he noticed all the Lasalle's Curiosity Shop brochures were missing — again. "I don't believe it. They're all gone. Something fishy is going on. Let's get back to the shop. I want to tell Will about this. And we need to find out what happened to the Lundys' wallet."

CHAPTER 6

Another Disappearance

The Aldens walked back quickly to Lasalle's Curiosity Shop. They passed T-shirt shops, ice-cream stands, and souvenir shops, but they didn't look in any of them. All they could think about was Mr. Lundy's wallet and the missing brochures.

"Police cars!" Jessie cried, as soon as they turned onto Waterfall Street.

The four children ran to see what the flashing lights were all about. When they reached Lasalle's Curiosity Shop, they saw a small group of people gathered on the sidewalk. The Aldens overheard bits of conversation.

"It's worth a fortune."

"I heard the Lasalles inherited it from a relative — someone who owned a hotel a long time ago."

"I always thought there was something suspicious about Angus Drummond."

"Angus!" Violet said to her brothers and sister. "I hope he's okay. Look, there's his suitcase on the sidewalk. But he's not sitting in his chair!"

"Would you tell me where Angus Drummond is?" Henry asked a police officer.

"That's what we'd like to know," Robert McKenzie said before the police officer could answer. "He was working with you children this morning. Then you left him in the display room by himself. Now the Prince of Wales guest book is gone, and so is Angus Drummond."

Jessie was shocked. "But he left his things here." She bent down to close the suitcase of old barrel chips. "He'll be back. Angus wouldn't steal anything."

Even the police didn't want to believe that Angus had the missing guest book. One officer turned to Robert McKenzie. "Angus Drummond is an old-timer around Niagara Falls. He can be a bit of a bother, but he's never caused any trouble, Mr. McKenzie."

Robert McKenzie didn't want to hear this. "I tell you, he was in the display room alone. After he left, the guest book was gone. It seems to me that he's your suspect."

The officer spoke to the Aldens next. "Is it true you left Mr. Drummond in the room with the guest book?"

Jessie swallowed hard before she answered. "I did. I'm so sorry. Will Lasalle said Angus was welcome in the shop anytime. Mr. and Mrs. McKenzie were right in the next room. I didn't think there would be a problem."

"Is Will here?" Henry asked. "He'll tell you that Angus is welcome in the shop all the time. He even helps the Lasalles with their collection. The Lasalles have known him for a long, long time. Just ask Will."

Sally McKenzie joined her husband. "Will isn't available right now." She paused. "I'm sorry. He's just not here."

The police officers didn't know quite what to do. "Mr. Lasalle will have to file a report about the value of the guest book. We can't do anything much until we get that — except keep an eye out for Angus. Maybe you can take this beat-up suitcase and this chair of his inside. If he returns for them, give us a call."

Henry and Jessie picked up Angus's suitcase and folded his chair.

Robert McKenzie reached for the chair and suitcase. "I'll take those. There have been enough mix-ups already."

After the police left, the Aldens followed Mr. and Mrs. McKenzie into the shop. Everyone was quiet. The children headed toward the display room.

Robert McKenzie blocked the way. "Sorry. This room stays locked until Will Lasalle gets back. It should have been locked when you left this afternoon."

Jessie sighed. "It's my fault. I'm sorry I

left Angus in there. I thought it was okay since I locked the back door and checked that all the cases were locked, too."

The children went outside to talk, away from the McKenzies. "We'll get to the bottom of this, Jessie," Henry told her. "And don't forget, we still have to find out about Mr. Lundy's wallet. We know Angus didn't steal that. Will locked it in the drawer. He and the McKenzies are the only ones with the keys. Let's go back in and ask them about it."

Henry went over to Robert McKenzie. "We ran into the people who lost that wallet I found, and — "

Before Henry could finish, Robert McKenzie broke in. "Wallet? There's no wallet here."

What was going on? Henry looked at Sally McKenzie. She fiddled with some papers on the counter.

"The wallet Mr. Lundy left behind in the display room," Henry explained. "Will said he keeps lost things in that drawer in case people come back. If they don't, he turns

them over to the Lost and Found Department at the police station."

Without looking up from the papers in her hand, Sally McKenzie spoke up next. "The police station. Yes . . . that's . . . uh . . . where we dropped off the wallet."

Even though Violet was usually quiet, this was too much for her. "The Lundys said there were no wallets turned in at the police station."

Before Violet could say another word, Robert McKenzie spoke up. "It's closing time. The police get a lot of lost items. They probably forgot all about the wallet. Now I have to let you out. It's getting late."

Henry would not give up. "When is Will coming back?" he asked. "Will can straighten out some of this."

"Not tonight, he can't," Mr. McKenzie answered. "We told him everything was under control. He's staying downriver with the Maid of the Mist crew for a while. We don't know when he'll be back. Good evening."

Robert McKenzie held open the back

door to the shop. The children had no choice. They left the shop without another word to the McKenzies.

"I wish Will were here," Jessie said when they went inside their bungalow. "He'd tell the police and the McKenzies that Angus has always been welcome in the shop."

Henry came over to his sister. "Don't worry. We didn't do anything wrong leaving Angus in the shop. The McKenzies are new to the shop, not Angus. If you ask me, they're pretty suspicious. On top of everything, they acted as if they'd never seen the Lundys' missing wallet."

Jessie sank back into the couch. The phone interrupted her thoughts.

"Grandfather? Oh, hello," she said when she picked up the phone. "We're so glad to hear from you. There was a theft at the shop. I think it was partly my fault."

The other children listened in. Jessie told Mr. Alden about the missing wallet and about Angus and the missing guest book, too. The Aldens took turns speaking with their grandfather. By the time they put down the phone, all of them felt a little better.

"Grandfather is right," Jessie told the others. "We just have to wait for Will to get back. Guess what? Grandfather called in dinner reservations for the four of us at the revolving restaurant in the tower — the one that overlooks the falls."

"Great!" Henry said. "That'll give us something to do to pass the time. I'm not hungry right now, but I bet we will be by the time we get to the restaurant."

At the thought of food, Benny finally perked up. "Tonight's fireworks night. We'll be able to see them while we eat."

The children decided to go for a walk until it was time to go to the restaurant. Waterfall Street was filled with people. When they passed the shop, the children saw the McKenzies arranging the display windows. They waved at the couple, but the McKenzies didn't wave back. Sally and Robert stared at the children. Robert McKenzie went over to the front door. He pulled down the shade. Lasalle's Curiosity Shop was closed.

CHAPTER 7

A Sky-High Mystery

Henry was right. By the time he and the other children arrived at the restaurant, everyone was plenty hungry.

"The falls are so pretty from way up here," Violet said when the Aldens stepped into the tower dining room.

"And you'll get to see our famous fireworks at nine o'clock," the restaurant manager said. "Just follow me to your table."

"I'm not dizzy at all," Benny said when the children were seated. "Are you sure this restaurant goes around?" he asked the manager.

"Once an hour," the woman said, smiling at Benny. "Just keep your eye on one fixed place in front of you. Soon you'll notice that it isn't in front of you anymore. This way you get a view of Horseshoe Falls and everything around it."

Sure enough, twenty minutes later, Benny was no longer looking down at the falls but at another tower across the way.

"Hey, this restaurant does move!" he said. "I'm glad it doesn't go too fast, or I might not be able to eat."

After the children ordered their dinners, Jessie decided to take snapshots of everyone. "I want Grandfather to have a picture of us in this restaurant."

Jessie reached into her backpack for her camera. Out fell the picture the Lundys had taken of the children at Journey Behind the Falls. "I forgot all about this," Jessie said. "We look so funny in those raincoats." She handed Henry the picture.

Henry studied the photo. "Hey, wait a

minute!" he said. "Look who else is in this picture. Isn't this the man we saw at the visitors' center?"

"The one who took all the brochures?" Jessie asked. "Are you sure?"

"Take a look," Henry said. "In this picture, it looks as if he's watching us. I'll bet it's the same person who left the group we were in."

Jessie examined the photo. She could see a tall blond young man in the background. "Maybe you're right, Henry. I'm not sure. I didn't get a very good look at him at the visitors' center. Anyway, why would he be following us?"

Henry shook his head. "Who knows? Maybe he wasn't. But it does seem odd that he keeps turning up in the same places as us."

"He doesn't look too friendly," Violet said when she looked at the photo.

Jessie stepped away from the table to take the picture. "Well, make sure to look friendly for this one," she said before she pushed the button.

After Jessie sat down again, dinner arrived. The waiter appeared with plates of crispy roasted chicken for Henry and Jessie. Violet and Benny had spaghetti and meatballs. Then the waiter explained that their grandfather had arranged to pay for the meal when he made the reservations. While the children enjoyed their good dinners, there were no more thoughts of the man in the photo. It was time to eat.

"Do you feel a little better, Jessie?" Henry asked after everyone finished dinner.

Jessie smiled. "Much better. I'm glad Grandfather arranged for us to eat in this restaurant. Everything looks really neat from up here, especially the fireworks."

By the time the Aldens were ready for dessert, the fireworks over the falls were over. The Aldens looked around at everyone in the restaurant enjoying their night out.

"Goodness!" Jessie whispered. "Look over there — not all at once, though." She nodded toward a table across the dining room.

"The McKenzies!" Henry said after he turned around ever so slightly. "What are they doing in this restaurant? I thought they had no money. I don't think Will could have paid them so soon that they could afford to eat here."

"Let's not stare," Jessie whispered. "I hope they didn't see us. Let's just look at our food and each other."

Benny had trouble doing this. "I can't just watch my peach pie. I have to eat it," he said to his sister. "But I'll keep my head down while I'm eating."

Violet gave Jessie a gentle nudge. "They're leaving now. I don't think they saw us. They would have said something."

Without looking up, Jessie whispered, "Let's follow them. We'll take the next elevator down. Maybe we can find out where they're going."

"Let's go!" Benny said. "A mystery is even better than dessert."

The Aldens caught the next elevator down to the lobby of the tower.

Finding the McKenzies didn't take long.

When the children stepped outdoors, the young couple was sitting in a horse and carriage, holding hands and smiling. They didn't see the Aldens.

"Now they look just like happy honeymooners," Violet said.

After the horse and carriage clip-clopped away, Jessie was puzzled. "I wish they *were* just happy honeymooners. What I can't figure out is where they got the money for the dinner in the restaurant. The horse and carriage ride costs a lot. Maybe they're spending money from the lost wallet. I hope they didn't take the guest book and sell it. After all, Angus wasn't the only one in the shop after we left. The McKenzies were there, too."

By the time the Aldens returned to the bungalow, they felt very tired. It had been a long day.

By ten-thirty all four were fast asleep. They didn't hear the first thumps down the back stairs of the shop.

But when there were more thumps, Jessie

sat up. "What's that, Watch?" she asked. But the Aldens' dog, Watch, was far away, back home in Greenfield.

Jessie saw moonlight coming in through the window. She yawned. "Oh, that's right. We're in Niagara Falls. Watch is at home." She pulled the covers tighter.

Another thump and some footsteps followed. Although it was chilly in the bungalow, Jessie slipped out of bed. When she looked out the window, she saw Robert McKenzie walk down the passageway next to the shop. He had a suitcase in each hand.

Jessie searched for her slippers but couldn't find them. Barefoot, she stepped outside just in time to see the McKenzies' car pull away.

"Too bad!" Jessie said, shivering in her pajamas. "They're gone." She turned back to the bungalow. In the moonlight, she noticed an envelope taped to the door. "What's this?"

She opened the envelope and read the note by the light of the moon:

Dear Aldens:

Tomorrow is Sunday. The shop will be closed all day. Will is coming back tonight. If you need anything you can call him. Robert and I have returned to the Rainbow Inn. We will see you Monday morning. You can take the day off.

Sally McKenzie

P.S. *Will left you these free tickets for rides on the Spanish Aero Car and the Maid of the Mist.*

Jessie checked the envelope. Sure enough, there were tickets inside. What a strange note to find so late at night.

Back inside, Jessie snuggled under the covers. There was no use waking up everyone. It would be morning soon enough. She would wait to tell her sister and brothers about the strange thumps in the night.

CHAPTER 8

High Above the Raging Waters

There were no more suspicious sounds outside the bungalow that night. The moon moved across the sky while the Aldens slept. Hours later, the morning sun awakened the children one by one.

Benny opened his eyes before the others. The first sound he heard was his growling stomach. *Time for breakfast,* he thought to himself, and tiptoed to the kitchen.

Benny poured cereal and milk into a bowl. Then he took out his old cracked pink cup and poured himself some orange juice.

By the time Benny finished, Violet was awake, too. "I had the strangest dream last night that someone came into the bungalow," she said as she walked into the living room.

Henry brushed his hair from his eyes when he came into the living room. "Know what? I had the same dream. I thought I heard something on the stairs, but there are no stairs in here."

Jessie jumped out of bed when she heard the voices. Joining her brothers and sister, she described seeing the McKenzies leave their apartment during the night. ". . . And then they drove away. When I turned around, I saw this note on the door. It said to take the day off. Will gave us free passes for the Spanish Aero Car and the Maid of the Mist."

"Goody!" Benny cried. "Can we go on the Maid of the Mist today, Jessie?"

Jessie knew there was no stopping Benny. "We might as well go on the Maid of the

Mist, since the shop is closed anyway. Let's have some breakfast. Then we'll head out."

Something bothered Henry when he read Sally McKenzie's note over breakfast. "Where did the McKenzies get the money to go back to the Rainbow Inn?"

"I wish we didn't have to think about that," Violet said. "They looked so happy last night in the restaurant and in the horse and carriage."

Jessie thought for a minute. "We don't know the McKenzies very well. Except for last night, they've always seemed so miserable. I don't understand why they refused to talk about the Lundys' wallet, too. I hope we get to know them better so we can figure out how they got more money. Now let's clean up before we leave."

After washing the dishes, the Aldens headed for the Maid of the Mist docks on foot. It was a beautiful day for a walk and a boat ride.

"The shops are just opening up," Violet said when the children stopped in front of an antiques store. "Look, they have some old Navy Island canes in the window, too. Angus was right. They really are expensive."

Benny pressed his face against the display window. "What I like are those old glass snowballs that have Niagara Falls inside. The ones now are made out of plastic."

Henry laughed. "You sound just like Angus Drummond, complaining about plastic souvenirs."

"I wish we could find Angus," Violet said. "I hope he's not in any trouble. Maybe we'll run into him today."

"Can we go into this store?" Benny asked. "Maybe Angus is in here. He likes old things."

The children entered the antiques shop. Except for a man talking to the clerk in back, the Aldens were the only customers.

Benny ran over to the display of glass snowballs. "Neat," he said when he got a close look at them. "Too bad they cost so much. I guess I'll just look."

As they examined the antique souvenirs, the children were very quiet. That's how they happened to overhear the salesperson talking to the other customer. "What do you mean, how much is the Prince of Wales guest book worth, young man? Mrs. Fustworth is off on the weekends, so I really couldn't say. In any case, an object like that belongs in a museum, not in a shop. We wouldn't buy or sell such a thing."

The Aldens hardly breathed. They wanted to hear every word.

"I don't want to sell it," the man said. "I just want to know how much it's worth. In the hundreds or the thousands?"

The store clerked cleared his throat. "I have no idea of its value. I've only been working here for a couple of weeks. As for the other items you asked about, you'll have to come back when Mrs. Fustworth is here. She does all the buying and selling. Is there anything in the store I can help you with?"

The man didn't answer. The next thing the Aldens heard was the front door slam.

"Come on, let's go!" Jessie said, halfway out the door. "We have to find out why that man was asking about the guest book."

Up ahead, the Aldens saw a tall blond

man dash across the street to a bus stop. He seemed to be in a hurry, and when a bus pulled up, he climbed aboard.

"Hurry! I'm pretty sure that's the man we've been seeing," Henry said. "Let's get on that bus." Henry stopped suddenly. "The walk light just turned red," he said, disappointed.

The Aldens were stuck on the other side of the street. Finally the walk light flashed again. Looking both ways, Jessie took Violet's hand, and Henry took Benny's.

"Now!" Henry raced to catch the bus across the street.

The children were out of breath when they reached the stop — just in time to see the bus pull away.

"We missed it," Jessie said. "Here comes another one. Maybe it'll catch up to the one that man is on."

After Jessie bought four passes, she and the other children took the seats right in front. They were going to keep an eye on the bus in front of them no matter what.

"You kids headed for the Aero Car?" the

driver asked the Aldens. “It’s quite a ride on a clear day like this.”

“Um . . . we’re not sure yet,” Henry answered. “Is that where this bus is going?”

“Oakes Garden, Great Gorge Adventure, Whirlpool Rapids, the power plant. You name it, I go there.”

As they traveled along the Niagara River Parkway, the Aldens held on to the safety bars of the bus. The other passengers looked this way and that at all the tourist spots along the route, but the Aldens never took their eyes off the bus ahead of them.

“Okay, let’s get off!” Henry said when he saw the tall blond man step off the bus in front of them.

“Thanks for the ride,” Violet said to the driver.

After the bus pulled away, the Aldens looked around. The whirling rapids of the Niagara River were far below.

“Is that man getting on the Aero Car?” Jessie asked.

Henry stood on his toes to see above the

crowds of people. "I think so. Let's get in line. We shouldn't be too far behind him since we already have our tickets."

"Hooray!" Benny said, though he made sure to take hold of Henry's hand. That Aero Car was awfully high above the water. The cable it traveled on was awfully skinny.

"It looks like the water is in a big mixing bowl down there," Jessie said. "Are you sure you want to take the cable car ride, Benny? We can wait here while Violet and Henry go on it."

"No way!" Benny answered. "I want to go, too."

The shiny red Aero Car was parked on a landing platform overlooking the gorge. The cable that would carry the car stretched above Whirlpool Rapids. The children saw the tall blond man in line ahead of them.

"The Aero Car is a lot like the cable cars we rode on in San Francisco, only the wheels are on top instead of on the bottom," Jessie explained to the younger children. "The cable slowly goes around a big spool. The wheels on top carry the cable car across the gorge."

"All aboard," a guide called out. "Whoa, stop right there," he said to the Aldens. "I have to do a head count. We're only allowed to let a certain number of people onboard."

The man counted the passengers already on the cable car.

Benny tugged at Jessie's sleeve. "Do you think we'll fit?"

"Okay," the guide said. "We can take four more. Go ahead."

After the door closed, the Aldens sat down in the last few seats. The tall man was on the other side, facing the opposite direction. The cable engine began to hum. The car glided slowly from the platform and over the raging water.

The Aldens didn't look at the water or even notice how high up they were. All they cared about was talking to the strange man. Did he know anything about the Prince of

Wales guest book? The Aldens meant to find out.

They peeked at the man as often as they could without attracting attention.

"I can't really see him," Benny whispered. "He's facing the other way."

"Just enjoy the ride," Jessie said. "It's really amazing way up here. We'll try to talk to him when we get off."

Benny wriggled in his seat. He just had to get a closer look at the man. There was one empty spot on the other side.

"Is it okay to change seats?" Benny asked the guide.

The man smiled at Benny. "Just as long as you don't rock the cable car or jump up and down."

Smooth as could be, Benny moved from his seat to the other side of the cable car. He heard Whirlpool Rapids swirling below. He tried not to look down, but he couldn't help it.

"Wow!" He took a deep breath when he saw the churning water.

Something else got Benny's attention,

and it wasn't the rapids. On the steep hill across the gorge, Benny saw something move. His feet froze in place.

"Benny?" Jessie called when she came over. "Are you dizzy? Come sit down again."

Benny started to speak, but his throat was dry.

"What is it?" Jessie asked.

Benny pointed to the cliff below. "Look," he said, "there's somebody down there. Doesn't it look just like . . ."

"Angus!" Jessie said. "He's climbing up that hill over there. Wait, I've got my binoculars in my backpack."

Jessie returned to her seat. She took out her binoculars. "It *is* Angus! Look." She handed the binoculars to Henry.

"It sure looks like him," Henry said when he spotted the bearded man making his way uphill.

The children shared the binoculars. What was Angus doing near Whirlpool Rapids?

By this time the Aero Car was on its way

back to the landing platform. The ride was nearly over.

"Let's get off first," Jessie said. "I don't like to push ahead, but we have to find Angus.

The Aero Car glided to a stop. The Aldens looked for the tall blond man among the other passengers.

"Should we split up?" Henry asked Jessie. "You could talk to that man while I search for Angus."

Jessie shook her head. "No, let's all go. Finding Angus is more important. Let's look for him across the gorge."

Violet squeezed Jessie's hand. "I'm glad we're going to find Angus. I know he has a good reason for disappearing."

CHAPTER 9

A Ride Through the Mist

The children looked across the deep gorge of Whirlpool Rapids. Now that they were back on the ground, the hill where they had seen Angus looked very far away.

"How will we get over there?" Violet asked. "Angus might be gone."

Jessie flipped through her guidebook. "It looks as if we can take a bus. One route loops around to the other side of the gorge. I hope it doesn't take too long."

But the ride did take too long. By

the time the children boarded one of the buses, ten minutes had passed. Ten more minutes passed while the bus moved slowly along the Niagara River Parkway.

"Finally," Henry said when the driver called out the stop. "I hope Angus is still over here."

The children ran to the viewing area at the top of the hill.

"Okay," Jessie said. "Here's where the Aero Car turned back. That means we're at the top of the hill where we saw Angus. I wonder if there's a path. The hill is pretty steep."

The children looked down the cliff. There wasn't a path in sight. Before they could explore any more, the Aldens noticed a park guard nearby.

"Let's ask him," Henry suggested. "Maybe there's a hiking trail to the bottom. After all, Angus got down there somehow."

The guard spotted the Aldens. He didn't look too pleased when he saw the four of them so close to the cliff. "Come away from there," he yelled out. "Stay behind this fence. There's loose rock."

"Sorry," Jessie yelled out. "Is there a path to the bottom of this hill? We're looking for somebody."

The guard raced right over. "Why? Did someone fall? I'll call headquarters. Give me the details."

Jessie shook her head. "No. No one fell. While we were riding the Aero Car, we saw a person we know climbing this hill. So we came back here to look for him."

"Impossible!" the man said. "No hikers are allowed beyond this fence. You can't climb this hill. There are no paths. No one goes down there. It's too dangerous."

Benny could hardly stand still. He had seen Angus with his own eyes. "But our friend Angus was down there. I saw him. We have to find him right away."

The guard rubbed his chin. "You don't mean Angus Drummond?"

Violet's face lit up. "You saw him, too? Tell us where."

"I haven't seen Angus since the police

were searching for him a couple days ago. It seems he may have stolen an old book or something," the guard said. "He used to have an old fishing shack down by the river. The park service made him tear it down, I think. Anyway, Angus couldn't get up and down these steep hills too easily."

Benny was practically jumping up and down now. "Yes, he could! He's like a mountain goat."

The man smiled. "Well, I could almost believe it. Anyway, Angus isn't here."

It was no use. The park guard wasn't going to let the four Aldens past that fence. If Angus was down by the river, nobody would know it.

"Too bad," Jessie said, while they waited for the next bus. "We lost the tall man. Now we can't find Angus."

Benny kicked at a pebble on the ground. "What do we do now that our adventure is over?"

"Who says it's over?" Henry pulled out his map. "Let's do what we set out to do in the first place. We'll go on the Maid of the Mist boat. The bus stops right there."

"Hey, it's the foursome," the bus driver said when the Aldens boarded another bus. "Don't tell me you kids have been riding around on the buses all morning. Why, there are dozens of other things to do in Niagara Falls, you know."

"We know," Benny answered. "We're going on the Maid of the Mist."

The bus driver smiled. "Well, you'll enjoy it. Now tell me. Did you folks ride the Spanish Aero Car?"

Benny couldn't wait to tell about his ride. "We sure did. And know what? When it got near the other side of the gorge, guess what?"

"What?" the driver asked.

"We saw our friend Angus Drummond climbing the big hill," Benny told the driver. "But the guard wouldn't let us go find him. It's too steep."

"You saw Angus Drummond?" the bus driver asked Benny.

"You know who he is?" Jessie asked. "Have you seen him?"

"Not today, but I saw him a few days ago," the driver said. "It wouldn't surprise me if he's down in that fishing shack of his somewhere. He moved it into the back-woods after the park service told him to take it down. Too close to the river, they said. If I see Angus, I'll let him know you're looking for him."

"Did you see a tall blond man?" Benny asked. "He was on that other bus."

"Hmmm," the bus driver said. "I get more than one or two tall blond men on my buses. I can't help you there. Okay, now, here's where you get off for the Maid of the Mist."

Soon the Aldens were in line for the blue raincoats all the Maid of the Mist passengers wore so they wouldn't get too wet.

"How do I look?" Benny asked when he posed for Jessie's camera a few minutes later.

"Look behind you!" Jessie lowered her camera and pointed behind Benny.

The other children whirled around. Just a few feet away stood the tall blond man from the antique shop. Like the Aldens, the man had on a blue raincoat.

The Aldens forgot all about their picture taking. They ran after the man and joined the same line of people boarding the *Maid of the Mist*.

"Sorry, full boat," the ticket taker told the Aldens.

Henry was quick. "We got separated from somebody. Can you let us on? Our friend, Will Lasalle, works on these boats."

Will's name worked like a charm. The ticket taker opened the gate and let on all four children. "All right. Just you four. Will's working in the engine room this shift. You'll see him somewhere on the boat, no doubt."

"Whew. We made it," Violet said, pulling on her hood. "I can already feel the mist from the falls."

The *Maid of the Mist* chugged toward Horseshoe Falls. The Aldens followed all the other tourists onto the deck. They wanted to get as close as they could to the roaring falls. They wanted to hear the roar. They wanted to get wet!

The children were not disappointed. Niagara Falls was closer, louder, and wetter than they had hoped.

"It's a good thing we have these raincoats!" Benny yelled. Nobody heard him over the roar of the crashing waters.

Finally the sturdy vessel turned away from the falls and headed back to shore.

"It's hard to find that man in this crowd of blue raincoat people," Henry said. "Let's go inside. Maybe we can find Will."

The children didn't take long to spot Will Lasalle.

"Will!" Henry shouted when they passed the engine room.

"Look!" Jessie said. "Will is in there with the man we were following."

Will didn't see or hear the Aldens. Their raincoats made them look like all the other tourists. The loud hum of the boat's engines and the waterfalls churning in the background drowned out everyone's voices. But the Aldens didn't need to hear Will to understand what was going on. They could see

that Will and the tall man were arguing. In a few minutes, when the boat engines quieted down, they heard the young men's voices, too.

"I told you not to come here when I'm working," the children heard Will say. "I've got work to do on this boat. I can't have you coming here or snooping around the shop when I'm so busy. Granddad already made up his mind. You had your chance to run the shop, Michel."

The children looked at each other. Where had they heard that name?

"Will is so upset," Violet said. "I wonder why that man is bothering him."

"I know. Michel is Will's cousin," Jessie said. "He mentioned his cousin Michel to Grandfather. They're in some of those old photos Grandfather showed us. Remember?"

Henry smiled. "Right! Will was the dark-haired cousin and Michel the light-haired one."

"But why are they fighting if they're cousins?" Violet asked.

"Let's find out what this is all about," Jessie whispered when Will's and Michel's voices grew even louder.

"I'm telling you, I didn't take the guest book," Michel Lasalle said. "Maybe Angus Drummond took it. And what about those people you hired instead of me? Complete strangers. How do you know they didn't steal Granddad's guest book?"

"You had the keys," Will said. "And you admit you put those fliers on the cars to make everybody think Granddad's shop was closing. And taking away all the brochures we need to advertise the shop. You did all that. Why should I believe you didn't steal the guest book to make me look careless?"

The Aldens heard nothing but the humming engines for a few seconds.

"I'm sorry, Will," Michel Lasalle said. "I just thought if it looked like you weren't doing a good job, Granddad would hire me back. He doesn't think much of me. But you . . . he'd rather have you part-time than me full-time. I wanted to make you look bad."

"Thanks a lot! You did a good job of it," the Aldens heard Will say before they heard a door slam.

"Hey! What are you kids doing here?" Will asked when he and Michel came out of the engine room. "I didn't know you were on the boat. I wish I could talk or give you a tour, but I'm too — "

"Upset," Henry said, finishing Will's sentence. "We overheard you and your cousin talking. We've been following him around Niagara Falls today. We've thought he was up to no good since the first day we got here."

Michel Lasalle interrupted, "Why have you been following me? Why is my business any of your business?" he asked the Aldens.

"Because we believe you took the Prince of Wales guest book, that's why. We heard you ask the man in the antiques store what it was worth," Jessie said, not at all afraid to speak her mind.

Everyone stared at Michel Lasalle. No one spoke for the longest time.

Will spoke to his cousin in a quiet voice. "Did you try to sell the guest book, Michel? You've got to tell me."

"No," Michel answered. "I promise you, Will, I was just trying to learn more about Granddad's collection. I don't have the guest book."

Will stared at the Aldens, then at Michel. In a low voice, full of hurt, he spoke to his cousin. "Then who does?"

CHAPTER 10

Yours Till Niagara Falls

By the time the Aldens left the docks, Will and Michel Lasalle had calmed down. The children decided to head back to the bungalow.

This time there were no flashing lights or police cars when they turned onto Waterfall Street. Crowds of tourists filled the streets. People went in and out of the restaurants and shops. But on this busy weekend, Lasalle's Curiosity Shop was still closed.

There was another note for the children

on the door. Henry tore it open. "It's from Grandfather. He came back a couple days early. He says to meet him at the Rainbow Inn as soon as we can get there."

The children fetched their jackets from the bungalow. The Rainbow Inn was just a few blocks away.

"There's Grandfather's car," Violet said when they reached the inn.

"There's another familiar car." Jessie pointed to an old brown car nearby. "Is that the McKenzies' car?"

"It is," Violet said, looking in the window of the car. "There's confetti on the floor. It's probably from their wedding." Violet paused. "I sure hope it doesn't turn out that they took the Lundys' wallet."

"Or the guest book," Henry added.

The children found their grandfather right away. He was enjoying a cup of coffee and the afternoon newspaper in the lounge area.

"There you are," he said, getting up to hug his four grandchildren. "You got my note. I figured you were out sightseeing around Niagara Falls. Tell me all about it."

The children settled themselves on a nearby couch. They told their grandfather everything that had happened while he was gone. It was easy to talk about all the fun things they'd done, like riding on the Aero Car and the Maid of the Mist. But it was harder telling him about the Lasalle cousins.

Mr. Alden looked upset when he heard the news. "I'm sorry to hear that Will and Michel Lasalle are not getting along. I'd heard Michel was careless when he worked at the shop. I hoped by now he'd grown up a little. Still, I don't think he'd steal someone's money. And certainly not his grandfather's valuable Prince of Wales guest book."

The lounge area was getting busy. The children had to speak louder to be heard.

Jessie was at the far end of the couch. She raised her voice so Mr. Alden could hear her. "We think the McKenzies may have taken the wallet, Grandfather. They knew where it was. Right after it was missing, they seemed to have a lot of money. We saw them at the tower restaurant. They're even staying here."

Jessie felt Henry tap her arm.

"Shhh," Henry said. "The McKenzies were sitting right behind us. I think they overheard us talking about them."

When the children looked up, they saw the McKenzies rush from the lounge. The young couple stopped at the front desk, grabbed two suitcases, and left.

"Can we follow them, Grandfather?" Henry asked. "I have a feeling they know all about the wallet. And maybe about the guest book, too."

Mr. Alden was out of his chair in no time. The McKenzies' car was just pulling out when the Aldens got into their own car. Mr. Alden followed the brown car down the street and onto the Niagara Parkway. He drove a couple of car lengths behind them.

"They're turning onto Peace Bridge," Jessie said a few minutes later. "What if they're leaving Canada?"

Mr. Alden pulled over next to a long

line of cars waiting to pass at the customs booth on the American side.

"I'm going to get a customs officer," Henry said. "Then the McKenzies will have to stop."

After Mr. Alden stopped, Henry went off to the customs booth. The other children got out of the car and walked over to the McKenzies' car.

Jessie knocked on the window. The McKenzies didn't roll it down or even look at the Aldens.

"We need to talk to you," Jessie said through the glass. "Just to ask a couple of things. Please talk to us."

Violet tugged on Jessie's sleeve. "Look what's lying on the backseat."

Jessie took a look. A large brown envelope lay on the backseat. On the front of the envelope, Jessie saw the Lundys' name and address printed in big black letters.

A minute later the customs officer arrived. He waved over the McKenzies' car. Now they had to roll down the car window.

"I understand you might have some stolen property," the officer said to the McKenzies.

Robert McKenzie looked pale. He picked up the envelope from the backseat and handed it to the customs officer. "The wallet in this envelope was missing but not stolen. Check inside. You'll find all the Lundys' money and identification cards. We were going to mail this to the owners."

"Sure, sure," the customs man said. "Well, I can't arrest you, since everything seems to be here. But I'll take this wallet now and get in touch with the owners myself. We want Niagara Falls visitors to know that folks here are honest."

"We are honest, just not too careful," Sally McKenzie said. "When the Lundys didn't come back for their wallet right away, I decided to take it to the police station. But I misplaced the wallet on the way. Honest."

Was Sally McKenzie telling the truth?

"Nobody knew us in Niagara Falls," she went on. "I was afraid we'd be accused of stealing the wallet and the guest book, too.

I tried to keep these children away until I found the wallet, which I did. It had fallen underneath the seat of my car. It's been here the whole time."

The customs man turned to the children. "Does this sound possible?"

The children wanted to say yes, but they couldn't.

"I don't like to mind your business," Jessie began, "but where did you get the money for the restaurant, and the horse and buggy, and the Rainbow Inn?"

Robert McKenzie answered that question. "Our old boss back in the States finally sent us our check. Since we were still on our honeymoon, we decided to spend the money on a few more nights in the inn and a nice dinner out."

The Aldens didn't know what to say next.

"We knew how bad it would look to everyone," he continued, "so we left Will a note that we were leaving. When we overheard you saying you thought we were thieves, we decided to leave Niagara Falls right away."

Sally McKenzie looked at the Aldens. "Why are you children smiling all of a sudden?" she asked.

Sure enough, the four children *were* smiling.

Violet was often shy, but not now. "We're just happy you got the money to continue your honeymoon after all."

Pretty soon the McKenzies were smiling, too — even Robert.

"I guess that means we can go back to the Rainbow Inn — and to the shop," Robert McKenzie said. "I want to tear up the note I left for Will Lasalle. We've got a job to finish."

Soon Mr. Aldens' car was on the Niagara River Parkway behind the McKenzies' car again.

"Look," Violet said. "They put their JUST MARRIED sign on the back of their car again."

"So they did," Mr. Alden said.

* * *

Everyone arrived at the shop just in time to see Will and Michel Lasalle pull up in front. The two cousins were smiling.

"I brought Michel along to give us a hand," Will explained to everyone. "From now on, he's part of the family business, too. Michel, meet Sally McKenzie. The man unlocking the door to the shop is her husband, Robert. This young couple has been a big help managing things around here."

"Hi, there," Robert said quickly. "I'll let you inside in just a second."

By the time the two cousins stepped into the shop, Robert had crumpled up his good-bye note and turned on the lights.

"Sally and I will be glad for your help," Robert told Michel. "The Aldens here are in charge of the display room, but from now on we all work together. No closed doors around here. I have a hunch if we all put our heads together, we can figure out what happened to the guest book."

"Look!" Jessie cried when the children entered the display room. "We don't have to figure out what happened to the guest book. It's back in the case!"

Everyone crowded around the glass case. Sure enough, the guest book lay open to the page with the Prince of Wales's signature.

Will and Michel looked over the children's shoulders.

"It's on a wooden stand," Will said. "A wonderful, carved wooden stand. How on earth did that get here?"

Only one person could answer that question.

Angus Drummond stepped from the shadows in the corner. "That stand is older than anything or anyone in this room," Angus told everyone. "Older than me, even. My great-grandma worked in the old hotel when the Prince of Wales visited there in 1860. She waited on the Prince and his family the whole time they were in Niagara Falls. When the hotel went out of business years later, my pa bought some hotel sou-

venirs at the auction. The Lasalles got the guest book, but the Drummonds got the stand the guest book was on."

Will couldn't believe it. "That's fantastic, Angus. I knew both our families were connected to the hotel. But I can't let you give this stand away. It belongs to your family."

Angus took a Navy Island cane and rapped it on the floor. "Who said anything about giving it away, young man? Not me. No, sir. You can borrow the stand for as long as this place stays open. Just make sure everybody knows it came from the Drummonds, that's all."

The Aldens were curious.

"Why did you take the guest book? And when?" Henry asked.

Angus tapped the floor with the cane again. "I didn't take the guest book. I borrowed it to see how it would look on this stand. Will's grandpa gave me a key to the display room a long time ago. He said I could go in anytime, so I did. But then you kids showed up before I could borrow the guest book. When I saw you, I went right out the front door and to my spot across the street, cool as you please."

"So it was you that first day," Jessie said. "You were quick."

"Well, I've been climbing the hills around Niagara Falls for a lot of years," Angus said. "I finally got hold of the guest book the day the McKenzies started work. All I wanted to do was look up some names from the olden days. I couldn't do that with everybody snooping on me, now, could I? So I borrowed the book. Pretty soon everybody's gone off their heads about it. The book was safe and sound the whole time."

The Aldens just had to know something else.

"We saw you on a hill near Whirlpool Rapids this morning," Henry began. "At least we think it was you. What were you doing there?"

Angus smiled. "Same thing I always do there — visiting my fishing shack in the woods. My shack was a good place to look at the book in peace."

Everybody looked relieved.

"The book is back now," Will said. "That's all that matters. And everybody can see the Prince of Wales's signature even better now that it's displayed on this stand. Thanks so much, Angus."

Benny wasn't the least bit interested in the guest book now that it was back.

"Hey, Benny, what are you doing?" Will asked when he saw Benny writing something in a book on the counter.

"Signing this new guest book, that's what."

The children came over to see what Benny was up to. Everyone laughed when they saw what he had written: *Benny Alden was here!*

Angus Drummond laughed. "That'll be a valuable souvenir a hundred years from now!"

GERTRUDE CHANDLER WARNER discovered when she was teaching that many readers who like an exciting story could find no books that were both easy and fun to read. She decided to try to meet this need, and her first book, *The Boxcar Children*, quickly proved she had succeeded.

Miss Warner drew on her own experiences to write the mystery. As a child she spent hours watching trains go by on the tracks opposite her family home. She often dreamed about what it would be like to set up housekeeping in a caboose or freight car — the situation the Alden children find themselves in.

When Miss Warner received requests for more adventures involving Henry, Jessie, Violet, and Benny Alden, she began additional stories. In each, she chose a special setting and introduced unusual or eccentric characters who liked the unpredictable.

While the mystery element is central to each of Miss Warner's books, she never thought of them as strictly juvenile mysteries. She liked to stress the Aldens' independence and resourcefulness and their solid New England devotion to using up and making do. The Aldens go about most of their adventures with as little adult supervision as possible — something else that delights young readers.

Miss Warner lived in Putnam, Connecticut, until her death in 1979. During her lifetime, she received hundreds of letters from girls and boys telling her how much they liked her books.

We're Taking a Trip!

Where can you go to find perplexing puzzles, great games, and amazing activities? Relax. You don't need a map to find your way. You're already here! This is the spot for some amazing vacation fun! And all of the puzzles, games, and activities come straight from the Boxcar Children themselves. No one knows fun like the Aldens!

To start the fun and games turn right — right to the next page, that is!

The Puzzle Place!

There are some really tough puzzles on these next few pages. But we know you can do it. You can check the answers to all the puzzles on the last two pages of this section.

Souvenir Search

Welcome to Lasalle's Curiosity Shop. Violet is looking for just the right knickknack to take home.

Study the picture. See if you can find these ten things: A log from a hermit's cabin, a photograph of Niagara Falls, an "I Love Niagara Falls" T-shirt, a Niagara Falls snow shaker, a walking stick, a Niagara Falls photo album, a jar of real Niagara Falls water, a Niagara Falls coin purse, a ship in a bottle that says "Maid of the Mist," and a Niagara Falls salt and pepper set.

Benny's Barrel

Benny didn't have any trouble finding his souvenir. He bought a piece of wood. The wood is special because it is part of a barrel a daredevil woman once used to go down the falls. Can you figure out which piece of wood Benny bought? Benny's piece of wood is the only one that would fit in the barrel's hole.

1 2 3 4 5

Through the Table Rock Tunnels

Wow! Henry has always wanted to go through the Table Rock Tunnels. They are beneath the falls. But now Henry has gotten lost in the tunnels. Can you solve this maze and get him out?

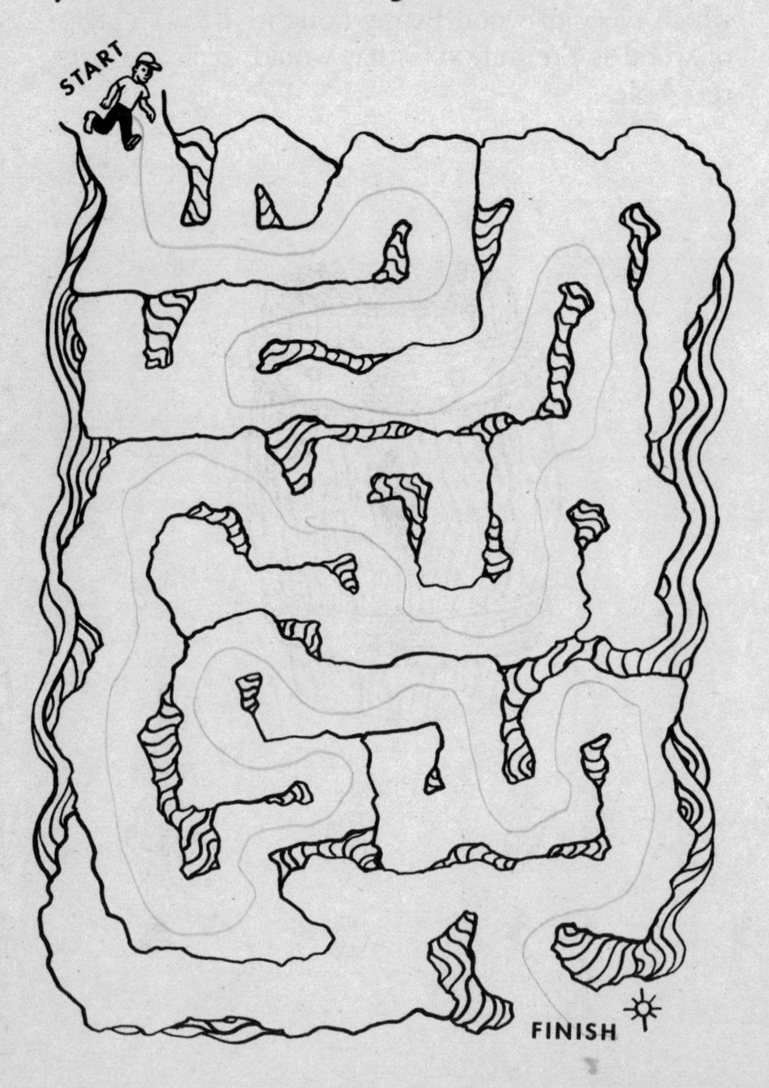

Cool Canada Word Search

Niagara Falls is a great vacation spot. And you can visit the falls in the United States or in Canada. The falls fall on both sides of the border! All of the words in this word search have something to do with our neighbor to the north — Canada. The words go up, down, sideways, backward, and diagonally.

Look for **COLD, ENGLISH, FRENCH, HOCKEY, MAPLE, MOUNTIES, NIAGARA, O CANADA, ROCKIES, SYRUP**

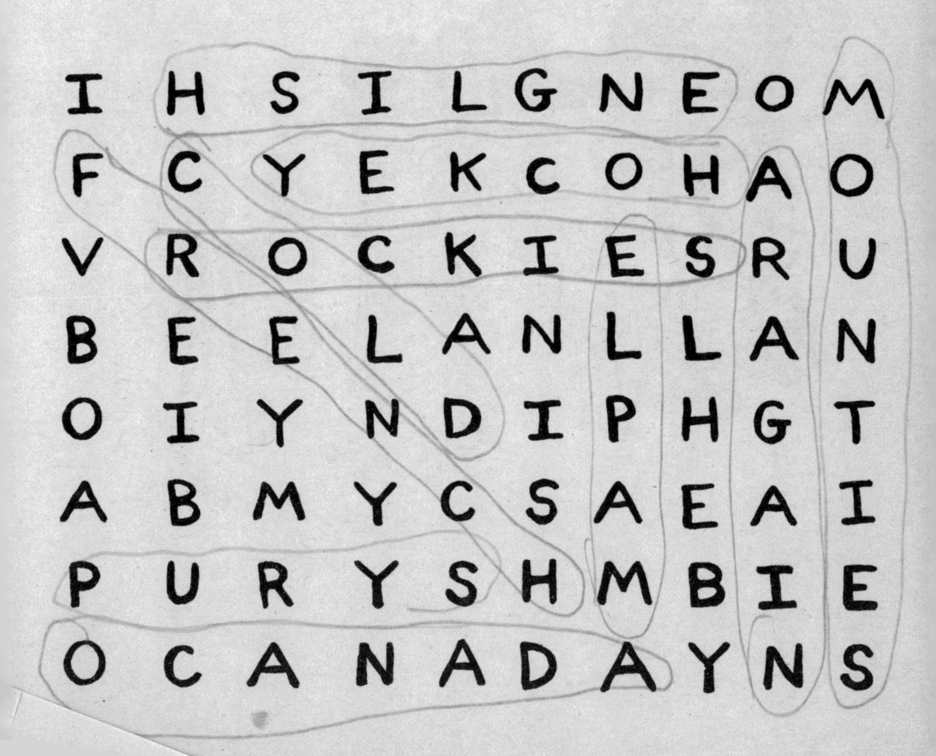

Photo Finish

What vacation would be complete without taking photographs? The Alden kids love taking pictures. Here are two pictures of the same spot. Jessie took one. Violet took the other. Can you spot the differences between the two pictures?

POPCORN

Yummy Car Snacks

It was a long car ride to Niagara Falls. And as everyone knows, Benny Alden cannot go a long time without eating. So the Aldens all got together and whipped up a few car snacks for him to take on the trip. Here are a few of their favorite recipes.

Corn Crunch

You will need:
$^{1}/_{2}$ cup butter or margarine
$^{1}/_{2}$ cup brown sugar
3 quarts popcorn
1 cup mixed nuts
baking pan

Here's what you do: Let the butter come to room temperature. Beat the butter together with the brown sugar. Mix in the popcorn and nuts. Spread the whole mixture evenly in a baking pan. Ask an adult to preheat the oven to 350 degrees. Then ask the adult to place the baking pan in the oven for eight minutes. After the mixture has cooled, dig in!

No-Cook S'Mores

You will need:
graham crackers
marshmallow topping
miniature chocolate bars

Here's what you do: Slather one side of two graham crackers with the marshmallow topping. Place a chocolate bar on top of one cracker. Then place the other cracker on top of the chocolate bar. Make sure all of the chocolate and topping is on the inside of your sandwiches.

Car Games

Are you one of those kids who is always asking the same question — are we there yet? So was Violet Alden — until she discovered these fun car games. Now riding in the car is one of the best parts of her vacation!

Silly Story Time

Choose one person to start. The first player begins a story. He can talk for as long as he wants. Once he stops, the second player takes up the story where the first left off. Keep going until everyone in the car has had a chance to add to the story. With so many people putting in their ideas, the story is sure to get sillier and sillier!

Ghost

The object of this game is *not* to finish a word. The first player says a letter. The second player adds a letter to that. All of the players go around and around, making a word, but trying not to be the one who finishes it. The player who does finish the word gets the letter G. If she finishes the next word, she gets an H, and so on until one player has finished five words and received the letters G-H-O-S-T. The players never know what the finished words will be. It depends on which letter each player chooses.

A player can also receive a G-H-O-S-T letter if he or she adds a letter to the word in play that does not belong in any word. For instance, say it is the second player's turn. He is faced with L-E-M. He adds the letter B. The third player cannot think of any word that starts L-E-M-B, so he challenges the second player. If the second player cannot come up with a word that begins with the letters L-E-M-B, he receives a letter in the word G-H-O-S-T. Once a player has earned G-H-O-S-T, he or she is out of the game. The winner is the last player left in the game.

Benny Alden's Favorite Vacation Jokes

Nobody loves a good joke better than Benny Alden. He knows that laughing is the best way to pass the time during a long car ride. So the next time you're on your way to a vacation spot, why don't you tell some of Benny's favorite vacation jokes. They're guaranteed to make the trip go faster!

Where did the hat maker go on her vacation?
The Kentucky Derby!

Why did the watchmaker take a vacation?
He needed to unwind.

How did the dentist like his beach vacation?
It was very en-jaw-able!

Did you have fun with cows during your ranch vacation?
No, it was an udder disaster!

Where did the wave go on her vacation?
To the shore!

Five Fun Facts About the Falls

Did you know . . .

. . . The Niagara Falls provide the greatest single natural source of water power in North America? The falls supply water to homes and businesses in Ontario, Canada; New York; and Pennsylvania!

. . . Niagara Falls carries about 500,000 tons of water per minute from one level of the Niagara River to another!

. . . The Rainbow Bridge links Niagara Falls, New York, to Niagara Falls, Ontario!

. . . Niagara Falls is such a popular attraction for newlyweds that the region is known throughout North America as "Honeymooner's Paradise"!

. . . Scientists believe the falls are 20,000 years old!

Puzzle Answers

Souvenir Search:

Benny's Barrel: Number four is an exact match

Cool Canada Word Search:

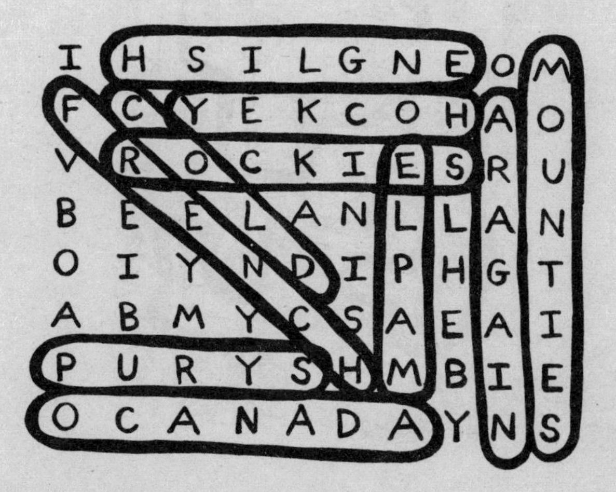

Through the Table Rock Tunnels:

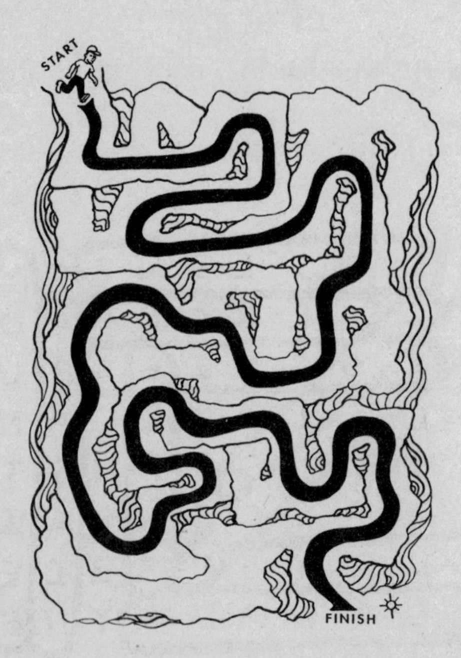